PRINCE IVAN
AND THE FIREBIRD

Всё ула́дится с тече́нием вре́мени

In the course of time, everything will come out right.

OLD RUSSIAN PROVERB

For Natasha

A TRELD BICKNELL BOOK

Published by Whispering Coyote Press Inc.
480 Newbury Street, Suite 104, Danvers, Massachusetts, 01923
Text and illustrations copyright ©1993 by Bernard Lodge
All rights reserved including the right of reproduction
in whole or in part in any form.

Printed in Singapore for Imago Publishing

10 9 8 7 6 5 4 3 2 1
This paperback edition published 1996.

Cataloging-in-Publication Data
for this book is available from
the Library of Congress.
LC # 93-12343

ISBN: 1-879085-63-1

PRINCE IVAN
AND THE FIREBIRD

A Russian folk tale retold and illustrated by Bernard Lodge

Whispering Coyote Press Inc./Boston

Long ago in a land of ice and snow there lived a king with his queen and their three sons: Prince Alexis, Prince Vladimir, and the youngest, Prince Ivan. The king dearly loved his queen and his three sons but, to tell the truth, more than anything else he loved a tree—a very special tree on which grew apples of solid gold, even in the depth of winter. With this rich harvest the king had covered with gold the hundred domes of his city.

But one morning disaster struck the kingdom. The palace guards were shocked to find that some of the golden apples were missing while others lay half eaten on the ground.

"Who has done this?" cried the king angrily. He ordered his guards to watch the tree more carefully the following night. But in the morning more apples were missing. The king then commanded each of his three sons to take turns guarding the tree. First, Prince Alexis stood guard. In his coat he carried a bottle, and he drank from it now and then to keep out the cold. It also made him drowsy and in the morning more apples had gone.

Next it was the turn of Prince Vladimir. He soon found his guard duty boring but he had brought along a pack of cards, so he amused himself playing solitaire. While Vladimir played, the thief was busy in the tree.

Then came the turn of youngest son, Prince Ivan.

Ivan was determined to stay awake,
so he rubbed snow in his face whenever
he felt sleepy. A few minutes before
midnight he heard a rustling sound, and
there high in the tree, he saw a strange
flame-colored bird pecking at one of the
golden apples. Ivan climbed the ladder

carefully rung by rung, but as his hand
reached out for the bird it spread wide
its wings to fly away. Ivan grabbed at the
bird but lost his balance and fell down
into the snow. All he had caught was a
long flame-colored feather.

"Better than nothing," declared the king the next morning examining the feather. "Now we know that the thief is that notorious Firebird who flies about in search of gold. My sons, you must saddle your horses and set out to find this bird. Do not return without it!"

Obediently the three Princes set off on their quest. Outside the city walls each of them chose a different road. Prince Ivan remembered that the bird had flown towards the east, so he rode in that direction. On the second day of his journey both Ivan and his horse were so tired that he decided to stop for the night. He unsaddled his horse and, using the saddle as a pillow and his cloak as a coverlet, he fell fast asleep. That night he dreamed a strange dream of flashing eyes and sharp white teeth. In the morning he awoke to a sight even *more* frightening.

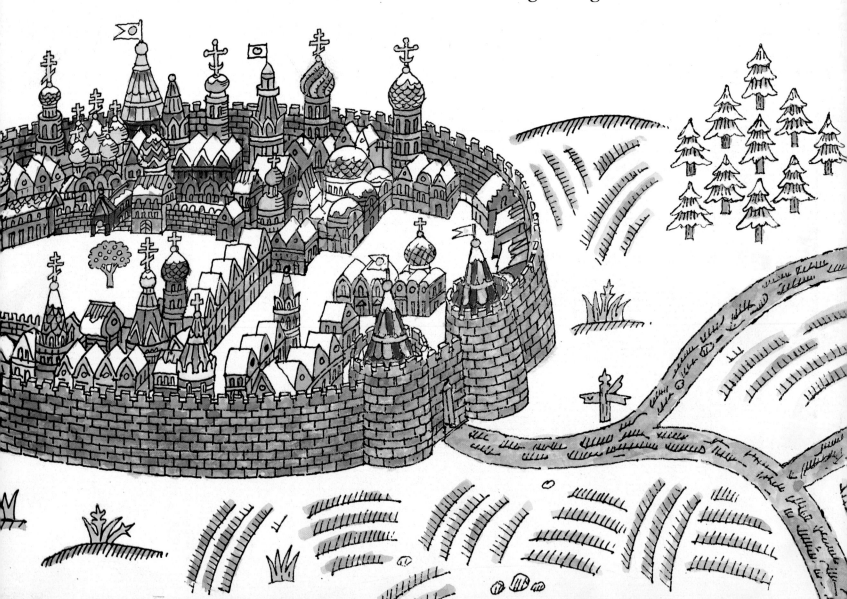

There, next to him, instead of his faithful horse lay a neat pile of bones, picked quite clean and white.

Ivan sank sadly to his knees before the monument of bones. As he did so a large gray wolf emerged from behind a rock.

"Why do you grieve so, Prince Ivan?" asked the wolf.

"Can you not see?" replied Ivan. "These bones are all that remain of my horse, the fastest animal on four legs."

"And very tasty legs they were too," said the wolf licking his teeth.

"So it was you!" cried Ivan, leaping to his feet and drawing his sword. The wolf laid a very heavy paw on Ivan's arm.

"Calm yourself, Prince Ivan. To kill me would be foolish. You seek the Firebird and I know the place where it lives. What is more, I can carry you there. After all, it is least I can do after making a supper of your horse last night."

Ivan was very angry and wondered if he could trust the wolf. But, since he now had no steed, he climbed onto the wolf's back and they set off together.

They rode far over mountains and frozen
rivers until they arrived one night at a
large rock that overlooked the City of
Wood.

"There," said the wolf. "In the tallest wooden tower you will find the Firebird in a golden cage. It is always set free one hour before midnight to fly in search of gold. You can easily unclasp the door of the cage but you *must not* attempt to remove the cage itself.

Ivan clambered over the wooden city wall and over many rooftops until he reached the tall tower. There, hanging like a bell in a belfry, was the golden cage. Inside it was the cunning Firebird. Ivan's hand moved to unclasp the door of the bird cage but, as his fingers touched the cage's beautiful ornate ribs, he felt a craving to possess it as much as the bird inside. Forgetting the wolf's warning, Ivan unhooked the cage. As he did so a clamor of bells rang out, lanterns were lit,

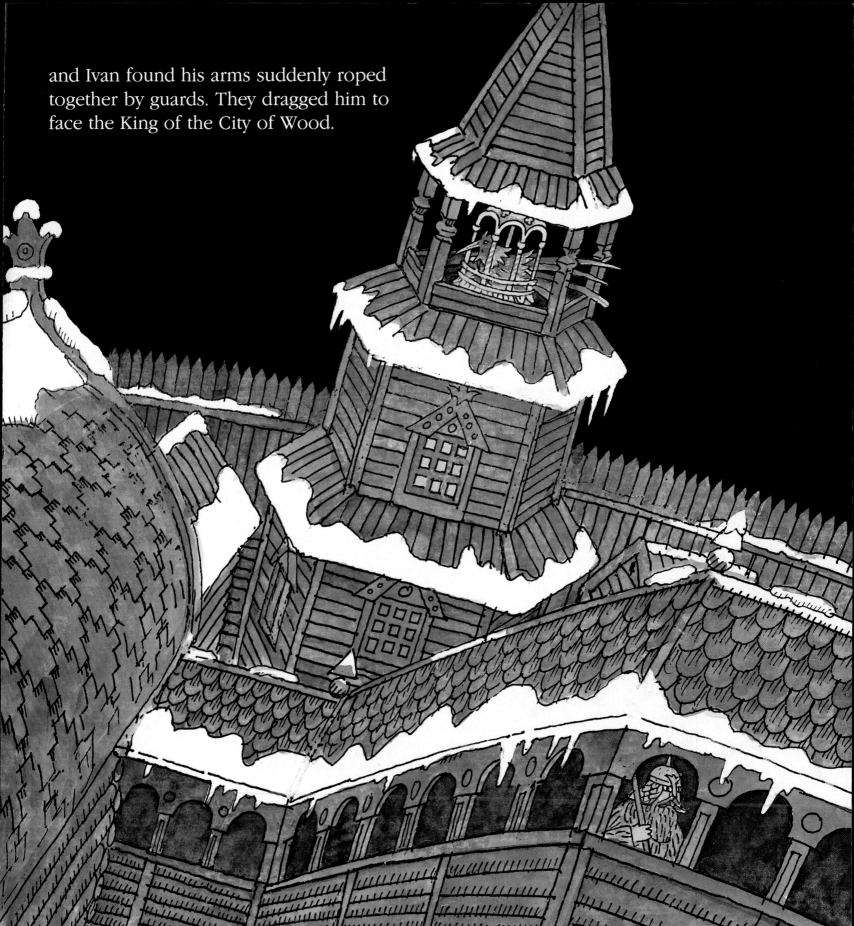

and Ivan found his arms suddenly roped together by guards. They dragged him to face the King of the City of Wood.

"Who are you?" demanded the king. He was shocked to learn that Ivan was a prince.

"Shame on you. If you had come to me as a prince and asked for the Firebird, I might have given it to you as a present for your father. Now the whole world will learn of your disgrace."

But then the king had an idea.

"Listen. Two days ride from here is the City of Stone. The king of that city owns a wonderful white horse with a mane of gold. Bring me that horse and, not only will I forgive you, but I will also give you the Firebird, cage and all."

Before Ivan could discuss the matter he was bundled out of the city. There, waiting in the snow, was the gray wolf.

"So," said the wolf, "you forgot to heed my warning about the cage and now you have entangled yourself in deeper trouble. But I promised to help you, so climb upon my back and I'll carry you to the City of Stone."

Off they went over hills and valleys until one night they arrived at the outer walls of the city.

"Now, Prince Ivan," said the wolf. "Listen carefully. In the center of the city, high up in the palace grounds, is the domed stable of the white horse. In the stable you will also see a beautiful golden bridle but I beg you not to touch it. There will be plenty of rope with which to secure the horse."

Ivan climbed over the stone city walls and over many stone roofs until he reached the Royal Stable. There stood the beautiful white horse. Ivan searched for a length of rope to tie around the horse's neck but his gaze fell upon the golden bridle. "It would be a shame to harness such a noble horse with an old rope," thought Ivan and, ignoring the wolf's advice, he slung the golden bridle around the horse's head.

At that moment the whole city awoke. Gongs boomed and a strange light filled the stable. Two giant guards lifted Ivan off his feet and delivered him—harnessed with rope—to the King of the City of Stone.

"Who are you?" thundered the king: He was shocked to learn that the horse thief was actually a prince.

"Shame on you and your family. Your wicked crime will soon be known throughout the world." But as Iván hung his head in shame, the king paused. He had an idea.

"Listen my royal horse thief, I will pardon you if you will perform a task for me. Less than two days' ride from here is the City of Silken Tents. The king of that city has a lovely daughter, the fair Princess Sonia. If you bring her to me the white horse, bridle and all, shall be yours."

Prince Ivan tried to explain that he had no wish to be entangled in yet another crime but the guards bundled him out through the city gates. The gray wolf shook his head sadly.

"Once again you have ignored my advice and now we are deeper in trouble. But climb upon my back and I'll do what I can to get us out of this mess."

Off they sped, far into the east, until one night they arrived at a valley in which stood the City of Silken Tents.

Now, Prince Ivan," said the wolf. "This time leave it to me. Wait over there behind that rock and I will fetch the fair Princess Sonia to you."

Ivan did as he was told and watched the shape of the gray wolf disappear into the shadows of a hundred silken tents. In no more time that it took for a large cloud to pass over the moon, the wolf reappeared and on its back sat the Princess Sonia.

Ivan's eyes opened wide because the princess was far more beautiful than her portrait had promised.

"Stop staring," growled the wolf, "and jump on my back before the alarm is raised." And the three of them sped off with Princess Sonia clinging tightly to

Prince Ivan for safety.

They were back at the City of Stone in less than two days, but in that short time, Prince Ivan and Princess Sonia had fallen in love. Ivan was heartbroken at the thought of handing the princess to the King of the City of Stone. The wolf took pity on them.

"Prince Ivan, you must hide your princess behind that bush while I turn myself into a likeness of her," said the wolf and began to chant:

Snout, tail, gray, gray hair,
I shall become a Princess fair.

He said it over and over until, in place of a shaggy gray wolf, there stood an exact replica of Princess Sonia.

Ivan led the wolf-turned-Princess into the city. The king was overjoyed and he gladly gave Ivan the wonderful white horse. Ivan rode out of the city to the hiding place of the real princess, lifted her onto the horse, and sped off for the City of Wood.

Meanwhile, back in the City of Stone, the king turned to embrace his bride-to-be but embraced instead a large gray wolf. The king fainted away and the wolf, leaping from the palace window, ran off to join his friends.

When he caught up with them he saw that Ivan was again very sad.

"Oh, gray wolf," said Ivan. "I cannot bear to trade this wonderful white horse for the thieving Firebird, yet I must take the Firebird back to my father."

"Don't worry," said the wolf, "our trick worked well just now. We'll try it again," and the wolf began another of his strange chants:

By my will and my deed,
I shall become a snow-white steed.

Princess Sonia hid the real white horse while Ivan took the wolf-turned-horse to the King of the City of Wood. The king gladly gave Ivan the Firebird in exchange and Ivan ran off to join his princess.

Courtiers helped the king to mount the wonderful white horse but he landed instead on the back of a large gray wolf. The king fainted while the wolf raced out through the city gates.

When the wolf caught up with his friends, Ivan said, "Now, gray wolf, you have repaid your debt and much more besides. How can I thank you enough?"

"Perhaps our adventures are not over, Prince Ivan," said the wolf. "But for now, farewell." And with that the wolf disappeared into the trees.

Prince Ivan, along with Princess Sonia, the white horse, and the Firebird, set off for his homeland.

They were no more than a day's ride from Ivan's city, passing through a dark forest, when two figures leapt upon them. As Prince Ivan struggled, he recognized his elder brothers, Alexis and Vladimir. Angry at having failed to find the Firebird, the elder brothers were now filled with jealous rage.

Ivan fought bravely and so did Princess Sonia, but they were finally overpowered. The jealous brothers tied Ivan to a tree.

"Good night, dear brother," said Alexis. "Sweet dreams as you freeze." And they rode off pulling the white horse with Princess Sonia and the Firebird close behind them.

Poor Ivan, now all alone and roped to a tree, watched the snow slowly fall. "Once again," he thought, "I find myself entangled, but this time there is no gray wolf to help me."

He had hardly said these words when a tug on his ropes and warm breath on his wrists told him the wolf had returned.

"Did you think I would leave you before you were safely home?" asked the wolf. "I know only too well your talent for landing in trouble. Climb onto my back once more and we will have the last

laugh." Then the two of them sped off in pursuit of Alexis and Vladimir.

The brothers had already reached the palace and were greeted with joy by the king and queen who heard all their lies and boasts. Why should they not believe them? The king decided they should celebrate immediately with a special feast.

They were seated in the great hall, with Prince Alexis sitting next to Princess Sonia and the Firebird displayed at one end of the table, when the doors of the hall burst open. In charged Ivan riding the big gray wolf. Everyone was

alarmed, but none more so than
Alexis and Vladimir.

"But we left you to freeze to
death," cried Alexis, and at that
moment the king and queen knew
how Ivan had been betrayed.

Princess Sonia was overjoyed to be reunited with her prince, and even the Firebird was pleased to see him, but the two wicked brothers were thrown into a deep prison.

Soon afterward Ivan and Sonia were married. It was a great ceremony followed by days of dancing and feasting. The gray wolf ate more than anyone else. Even the brothers were allowed out of prison for one day—but *only* to wash the dishes.

The Firebird was forgiven for stealing. It was kept as a pet and was allowed one golden apple a day.

So everyone—or almost everyone—was happy.